THE FOX
AND THE STORK

To Izzy, who loves foxes (and soup!)
Love Mum
L.K.

With love to Dave the un-foxable.
J.N.

Reading Consultant: Prue Goodwin, Lecturer in literacy and children's books

ORCHARD BOOKS
338 Euston Road, London NW1 3BH
Orchard Books Australia
Level 17/207 Kent Street, Sydney, NSW 2000

First published in 2011
First paperback publication in 2012

ISBN 978 1 40830 963 6 (hardback)
ISBN 978 1 40830 971 1 (paperback)

Text © Lou Kuenzler 2011
Illustrations © Jill Newton 2011

A CIP catalogue record for this book is available
from the British Library.

1 3 5 7 9 10 8 6 4 2 (hardback)
1 3 5 7 9 10 8 6 4 2 (paperback)

Printed in Great Britain

Orchard Books is a division of Hachette Children's Books,
an Hachette UK company.
www.hachette.co.uk

THE FOX
AND THE STORK

Written by **Lou Kuenzler**
Illustrated by **Jill Newton**

ORCHARD

Old Aesop was an Ancient Greek –
his AWESOME FABLES are unique.
Each fun tale gives good advice,
reminding us we must be nice.

Do not flick bogeys from your nose.
Always clean between your toes.
Wash your hands each time you pee.
Do not put bugs in Grandma's tea.

These things are said to help you out.
So listen up! Don't be a lout!'
Come and hear this Aesop fable –
follow me to Fox's table . . .

See how Fox, there, strokes his chin
and smiles a sly and foxy grin.
Beware! This beast plays wicked jokes
on all the other woodland folks.

He wrote a book called *You've been Foxed!*
(available in all good shops).
It tells of many tricks he played.
(Fox says a movie will be made.)

Fox once crept up on sleeping Hare
and shaved his ears completely bare!

Poured peppercorns down Badger's den –

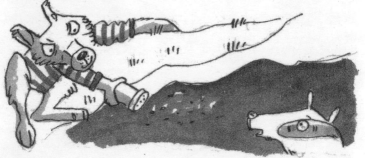

when Badger sneezed, Fox poured again!

He tied the tails of baby mice –
with six a bunch. It's just not nice!

Fox claims he is "Olympic champ"
at playing tricks. The rotten scamp!
But I can tell you that's not true . . .
There was *one* time his joke fell through.
Fox hasn't put this funny tale
into the book he has for sale.
He doesn't like it to be heard
that he was beaten by . . . a bird!
But now it's time for *me* to talk . . .
Yes, my friends, I am THE STORK!

Fox made a very big mistake
the day he saw me by the lake.
Flying south, I'd just dropped down –
a perfect stranger, new in town.

My beak and wings were icy blue,
from chilly winds I'd battled through.
"Hello!" said Fox. "How nice to meet.
Please let me fix a bite to eat.
You're shivering, Stork, like wobbly jelly.
I'll boil some soup to warm your belly!"

I'm smart, and fooling me is hard,
but fox had caught me off my guard
by acting like a perfect gent.
"Yes please!" and off he went.

Of course, I thought his smiles were kind.
I did not know he was inclined
to trick us all by playing pranks.

All I could think was: "How polite
to offer soup this chilly night."
He came and led me down the pier.

A table, set all clean and white,
was twinkling in the evening light.

Sit down, dear Storky. Feel at home.
How nice I will not eat alone.

A strange pair, us – the fox and stork.
We sat beneath the stars and talked.

15

Fox let me talk about my dream.
I did not see his dark eyes gleam.
I sat and shared my greatest hope . . .
While all along he planned his joke!
As I talked . . . how hungry I got!
A cunning part of Fox's plot!

With still no sign of soup in sight,
my guts were turning, twisting tight.
My empty tum began to groan,
a loud and gurgling belly-moan.

"Forgive me, dear." Fox hung his head.
"You must be hungry now," he said.
"My tasty soup, I'm sure you smell,
was left to cook and simmer well."
Fox was right. I could smell prawn.

My favourite chowder – nice and warm!

Of course, he knew the steamy pot
would smell delicious, rich and hot.
He called two moles, in velvet suits,
to act as waiters bringing soup.

A moment after that, the moles
staggered up with two flat bowls.
I hate to fuss (storks are polite),
but shallow dishes are not right.

"Tuck in!" A grin crossed Fox's face.
"Let's make this fun! Let's have a race!"

He lapped his soup in six quick slurps,
while I just sat there – like a twerp.
My bowl was filled right to the brink . . .
But still too shallow for me to drink.

I couldn't reach a single drop.
My rumbling tummy wouldn't stop!

"What's wrong?" smiled Fox. "Not feeling ill?"

The problem is my long thin bill.
I cannot reach the yummy soup.
Not even if I bend or stoop.

"Forget good manners," chuckled Fox,
licking soup from round his chops.
"Jump on the table! On your chair!
Eat how you like, and I won't stare."

I *still* thought Fox was being kind,
"I'll try," I said. "If you won't mind?"
I stood the dish between my feet . . .

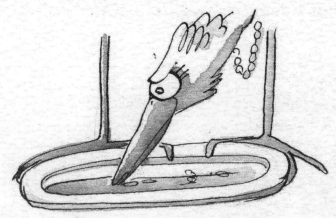

Then balanced it on my head to eat.
The flat bowl was completely wrong –
it didn't fit a beak so long.

The more I twisted, turned and wriggled,
the more that sly fox grinned and giggled.
I saw at last how cruel he'd been –
Fox was simply very mean!

The shallow bowls were Fox's trick,
knowing birds can't slurp or lick!

"Pity!" Fox said. "What rotten luck!"
And with six licks drank *my* soup up.
He licked both bowls completely clean,
then laughed about how sly he'd been.

"Sorry, dear, you missed your dinner.
You should eat or you'll grow thinner!"

I felt starved and most upset . . .
But wait! This game's not over yet!
Fox thinks he's sly and super smart,
but brainy birds can play their part!

"Don't fret," I said. "The meal was great!
I'll cook tomorrow – come at eight."
"Really?" Fox asked me, looking stunned.
All the same, he said he'd come.

"Don't eat breakfast!" Away I flew.
"I'm making very FILLING stew!"

Next day, I went to see the moles . . .

Fox never paid for serving bowls.
He promised us a handsome tip,
but it was just another trick!

"Don't worry, friends, my clever plot
will show old Foxy what is what!
He thinks I'm just a daft birdbrain –
we three will make him think again!
We'll see how hungry Foxy feels
when kept away from yummy meals."

I let a saucepan boil and bubble –
"Now *I* get to cause some trouble."

The smell of stew went through the wood,
all rich and smoky, warm and good.

Fox hurried down towards the lake.
Hunger made him drool and shake.
"I'm starved!" Fox said through
   dribbled spit,
"Your stew smells good. I want a bit!"

"Hello!" I said. "Pull up a chair.
The food is coming. Just wait there."

"Now, Moles," I smiled. "Bring us the stew. Served the way I told you to!"

The moles were really very small,
I thought they'd fall with pots so tall.
I'd served the stew in jars, you see.
No good for Fox. But great for me!"

I turned to Fox – my chance to grin –
"Why not get started? Do tuck in!"

Fox stared down, deep in thought.
He knew his nose was far too short.
There was no way his stubby snout
would fit inside the narrow spout.

"Please help," he begged. "This stew smells fine."

But I took his, like he took mine.
I put my beak inside his pot –
I slurped his stew and ate the lot!

"You've used my trick on me!" he said.
"I can't believe it!" Foxy fled.
We heard his tummy rumble loud
as he ran off, no longer proud.

I paid each mole a piece of gold.
Those tiny guys had been so bold!

We'll tell the wood of Fox's shame!
How clever Storky beat his game!

You see, one bad turn brings another.
Don't play cruel jokes or tease each other.
The Aesop lesson you should learn
is: horrid tricks are soon returned!

AESOP'S AWESOME RHYMES

Written by Lou Kuenzler
Illustrated by Jill Newton

All priced at £4.99

Orchard Books are available from all good bookshops, or can be ordered from our website, www.orchardbooks.co.uk, or telephone 01235 827702, or fax 01235 827703.